Harvey and Benny Play the Drums!

Story by Pamela Rushby
Illustrations by Omar Aranda

Contents

Chapter 1

A Drummer for the School Band

On their first day at school after the holidays, Harvey and Benny saw something interesting on the music room noticeboard. It was a flyer about a big band competition for all the schools in the city. It said there was a special prize for the best drummer.

"I wonder if our school will enter?" said Harvey.

"I don't know," said Benny. "There's a problem, though. Since Layla's family moved away, our school band doesn't have a drummer any more."

INTER-SCHOOL
BIG BAND
COMPETITION

The music teacher, Ms Chan, had overheard Harvey and Benny talking. "I do want us to enter the competition, so I need someone to learn to play the drums," she said. "Would either of you be interested?"

The drums! Harvey thought the drums could be fun. He put his hand up. So did Benny.

Ms Chan looked from one to the other. "We only have one drum kit," she said. "I'm happy to teach both of you, but only one of you will be able to play in the big band competition."

"The best drummer would get to take part?" Harvey asked.

"Yes, that's the idea," said Ms Chan.

"But we could both learn?" asked Benny.

Ms Chan nodded.

"That's all right, then," Benny said, smiling.

Chapter 2

Drumming Lessons

Ms Chan began to teach the boys to play the drums. They both loved it. They took turns to practise on the drum kit at school.

Ms Chan showed them videos of some famous drummers on the internet. The boys watched closely to see how the famous drummers played.

Sometimes, Ms Chan used her tablet to film the boys as they practised. Then they all watched the videos together to see what Harvey and Benny were doing right – and wrong.

One weekend, Harvey's Uncle Max came over for a mountain bike ride. Uncle Max, Harvey's dad and Harvey often went riding together.

"I hear you're learning to play the drums, Harvey," Uncle Max said. "Do you like it?"

"I love it!" Harvey said. "And I might get to play in a school big band competition."

"You know, I used to play the drums in a band," said Uncle Max. "Remember?" he said to Harvey's dad.

"That's right," said Dad. "You weren't bad."

"I still have the kit," said Uncle Max. "Would you like it, Harvey?"

Harvey couldn't believe it. "A real drum kit? Yes! Yes, please!"

Chapter 3

Let There Be Drums

Uncle Max came over to Harvey's house again a few days later. He opened the back of his car. "Here you go," he said. "Bass drum. Snare drum. Three tom-toms. And cymbals: hi-hat, crash and ride. The whole kit."

"Wow, thanks, Uncle Max!" said Harvey. "Where can we put it, Dad?"

"The garage would be a good place to practise," said Harvey's dad.

The next time they had a lesson with Ms Chan, Benny noticed that Harvey's drumming was getting better and better. "You must be practising a lot at home," he said.

"Uncle Max is helping me, too," said Harvey. "He's teaching me a really great drumming piece. I can show it to you on the internet. It's by a famous drummer called Sandy Nelson, and it's called 'Let There Be Drums'."

Ms Chan wanted to see the drumming piece as well, so the three of them watched it together on her tablet.

Then, Ms Chan filmed Harvey playing the piece.
"That sounded so good!" she said.
"It could even win the special prize for
the best drummer in the big band competition."

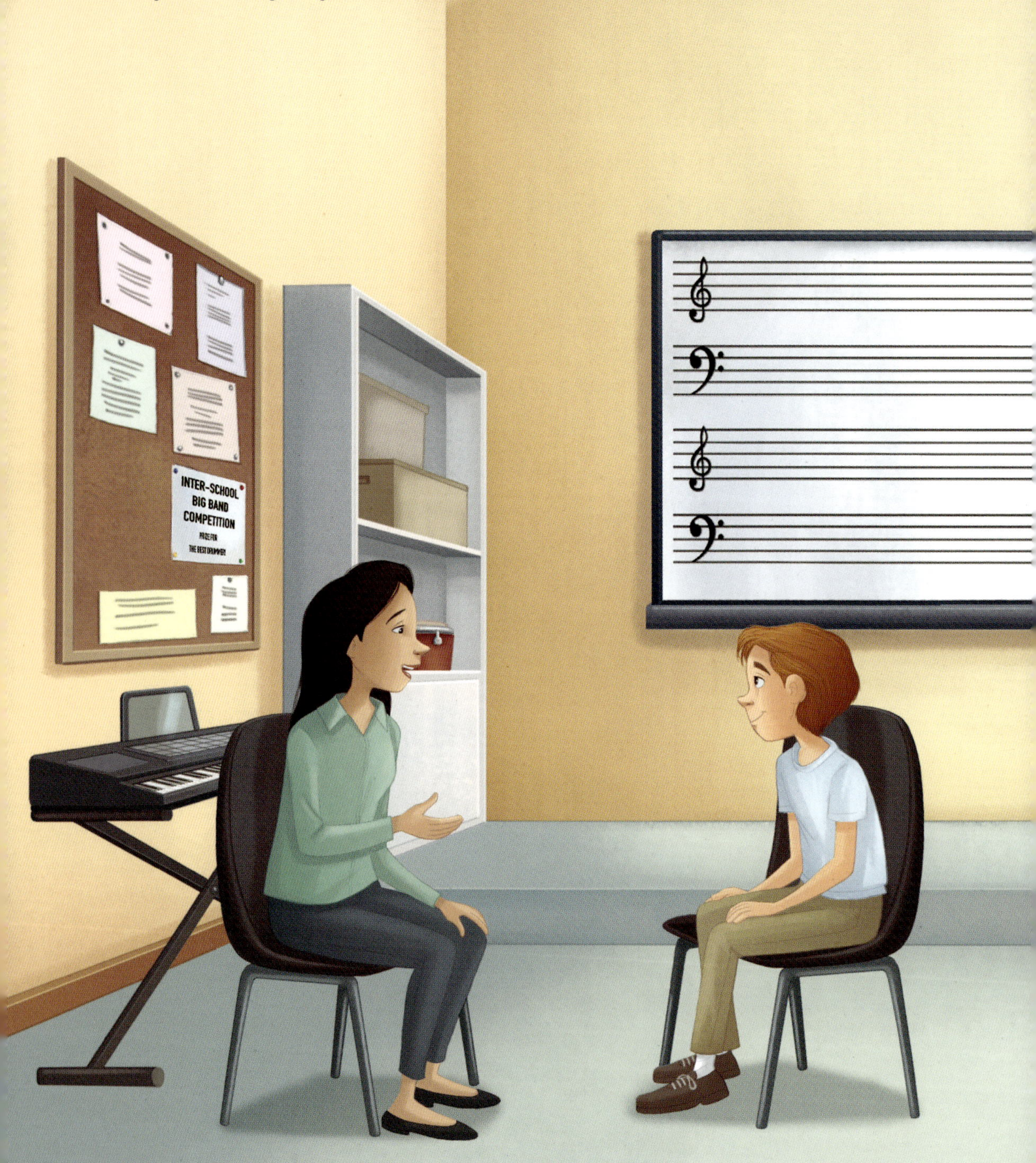
INTER-SCHOOL
BIG BAND
COMPETITION

Ms Chan asked Benny to stay back after their lesson. "The competition is very soon, Benny," she said.

Benny knew what Ms Chan was going to say. "You've chosen Harvey to play in the competition, haven't you?" he said.

"Yes," said Ms Chan. "I know you've worked hard, Benny, but . . ."

"But he's the better drummer," said Benny. "That's okay. I know he is."

Chapter 4

A Biking Accident

Benny was disappointed he wasn't playing in the big band competition, but that was just the way it was. Harvey *was* the better drummer.

Then, on Monday, Harvey came to school with his arm in a sling.

"What happened?" gasped Benny.

"I went mountain biking with Dad and Uncle Max," said Harvey. "I hit a rock and I went right over the handlebars. I've sprained my wrist."

“But the competition is next week!” said Benny. “Can you still play the drums?”

“No,” said Harvey. “It’ll be you.” Harvey was disappointed, but he still wanted his school to do well in the competition. “Come on,” he said to Benny. “Let’s watch the Sandy Nelson video again. Then you’d better do some practice.”

Benny practised hard all week.

“You’re sounding just like Sandy Nelson!”
Harvey encouraged him.

Benny grinned. “No, I’m not. But I hope
I’m a *little* bit like him.”
He knew he still wasn’t as good as Harvey, though.

Chapter 5

A Place in the School Band

The day of the big band competition arrived. It was being held at Harvey and Benny's school. Bands from other schools came to compete, and students from those schools and their families came to cheer them on.

The day began with the drummers from each school band playing solos. Benny watched the drummers from the other schools closely. His heart sank a little. He was pretty sure he wasn't quite as good as them. He thought Harvey was, though. If only Harvey could play! Benny was sure Harvey would have had a good chance to win the special drumming prize, if he hadn't hurt his wrist.

Then, Benny had an idea. He had a quick word with Harvey. Then he had a quick word with Ms Chan. Ms Chan had a quick word with the judges. Then, Benny and Ms Chan paid a very quick visit to their music room – and came back with Ms Chan's tablet.

One of the judges walked onto the stage. "Before we announce the winner of the special drumming prize," the judge said, "we have had a surprise entrant. One drummer hurt his arm and couldn't play today. But we can still see him perform – and here he is."

The lights dimmed, a big screen descended from the ceiling, and a video began to play. It was the video that Ms Chan had filmed of Harvey in the music room, playing "Let There Be Drums"!

The video finished.

The students from Harvey's school cheered.
The students from the other schools cheered too –
because Harvey was *great*!

The judges talked together, before announcing that Harvey had won the special drumming prize.

Then all of the bands, one after another, did their final big performances. Benny took his place as the drummer in his school band. He mightn't be quite as good as Harvey and some of the other drummers, Benny thought to himself, but he was there, playing in the school band.

And Benny was having a wonderful time!